Corte Madera Children's New
E Richards
You matter to me :
31111042941136

You Matter to Me

You Matter to Me

written by
Doyin Richards

illustrated by
Robert Paul Jr.

Feiwel and Friends
New York

A FEIWEL AND FRIENDS BOOK

An Imprint of Macmillan Publishing Group, LLC

120 Broadway, New York, NY 10271

mackids.com

Text copyright © 2022 by Doyin Richards. Illustrations copyright © 2022 by Robert Paul Jr. All rights reserved.

Our books may be purchased in bulk for promotional, educational, or business use.

Please contact your local bookseller or the Macmillan Corporate and Premium Sales Department at

(800) 221-7945 ext. 5442 or by e-mail at MacmillanSpecialMarkets@macmillan.com.

Library of Congress Cataloging-in-Publication Data is available.

First edition, 2022

Book design by Mike Burroughs

The illustrations were digitally rendered with SketchBook Pro. This was done to emulate

the vibrant nature of watercolors and the smooth touch of creamy pastels.

Feiwel and Friends logo designed by Filomena Tuosto

Printed in China by RR Donnelley Asia Printing Solutions Ltd., Dongguan City, Guangdong Province

978-1-250-83448-5 (hardcover)

1 3 5 7 9 10 8 6 4 2

This book is dedicated to my dog, Biscuit.
Thank you for loving me unconditionally through
the good times and bad. My world is so
much happier because you're in it.

—D.R.

To Leah.

—R.P.

Yeah, I know I'm cute.
But this isn't about me.
It's about him. You know . . .
my human, my guy, my homie.

I used to live in a shelter.

Even with other dogs there, I always felt alone.
Then my human locked eyes with me and told me I was the one.
Before I knew it, we were driving to my new home.

My human showed me my new fluffy bed.
I had a shiny food bowl! And toys to chew!

But I worried that it wouldn't last.
Would he send me back to the shelter?
I couldn't get comfortable here . . . or with him.

"I'll be honest,"
my human said.

"I've never had a dog before,
but I'm going to do my best to
make you the happiest pup ever.
I love you and you matter to me."

I didn't understand what he meant at first.

But as the days passed, my human would show how much he loved me and what it meant to matter.

When I was hungry—**BOOM**, he'd hit the kitchen and whip up some amazing grub for yours truly. (Some call that being spoiled. And they might be right.)

When I sometimes peed a little . . . in the house . . . by accident . . . my human didn't yell. He'd smile and say, "I used to pee in the house when I was a baby, too. You'll figure it out."

And I finally did.

Getting used to my human and new home took time.

But if I cried, got a case of the zoomies, or just wanted a lap to nap on, he was always there.

Put simply, my human is dope. But . . .

Sometimes when we go out together, other humans look at him as if he's scary. They cross the street to avoid him or clutch their bags tightly.

Other humans will stop to pet me,
but it's always about me.
They don't look at my human.
They don't smile at him.

They ask for my name, but not his.

Just because I can sense these things doesn't mean they make any sense.
He's my human.
Why doesn't everyone else see what I see?

I try to help. Whenever I see other pups on my walk, I wag my tail and play with them.

My human smiles.
The other humans smile.

Then they start talking to each other.
I can tell that makes my human happy.
At least for that moment.

Why are other humans afraid of him?

Why do other humans ignore him?

Every day my human tries to prove that he has a good heart and that he matters. He says it's like trying to empty the ocean with a spoon.

He's tired. He's broken. Just because I can sense these things doesn't mean they make any sense.

Because my human still shows up to be the best guy he can be. For his family, his friends, his clients, his community, and for me.

I see him. I support him. I love him. He matters to me.

Talk to him.

Smile at him.

Eat with him.

Watch sports with him.

Get to know him.

You'll realize that my human is just like you.

Until then, I'll walk by his side and protect him.

He rescued me, and now it's my turn.